Penelope Gets Wheels

by Esther Allen Peterson · illustrated by Susanna Natti

Crown Publishers, Inc. New York

Also by Esther Allen Peterson

Frederick's Alligator

10 9 8 7 6 5 4 3 2 1

The text of this book is set in 14 point Century ITC Book.
The illustrations were prepared by the artist with half-tone overlays, for black, red and yellow.

Library of Congress Cataloging in Publication Data

Peterson, Esther Allen.
  Penelope gets wheels.

  Summary: Penelope buys roller skates when her birthday money won't stretch to a car or bicycle, but they turn out to be the "best wheels a kid can have."
  [1. Roller skating — Fiction] I. Natti, Susanna, ill.
II. Title.   PZ7.P4434Pe   1982   [E]   81-7856
ISBN: 0-517-54467-9   AACR2

To Mary, Bob, Natalie, and Alyssa

E.A.P.

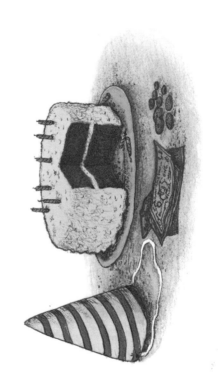

Penelope Gets Wheels

It was Penelope's birthday, and she got 10 one dollar bills,
4 quarters, and 5 dimes.

She counted the money many times, and it always came out
the same: $11.50.

"I am rich and I am older now," She said to her mom. "I don't need to walk anymore. I will go on wheels."

"Wheels?" asked her mom.

"Yes," said Penelope. "I would like a car, but I know I am not rich enough or old enough. I think I will buy a bicycle."

"A bicycle costs a lot of money," said her mom.

"I have lots of money," Penelope said. And before her mother could say another word, she ran outside and went to the nearest department store.

"Today is my birthday," she said to the saleslady. "I would like to buy that silver racing bike."

"That bicycle costs one hundred and nineteen dollars," the saleslady said.

Penelope pointed to a smaller bike. "How much is that one?"

"Seventy-nine dollars and ninety-five cents," said the saleslady.

"I'm not that rich," Penelope said, and she put the money back in her pocket.

Penelope looked at badminton sets, paint-by-number kits, and baseball bats and gloves. But she didn't want to buy anything she saw.

Then she saw some roller skates. They were $9.95 a pair. She picked up a skate and spun its wheels. "I guess these are all I can afford."

"That will be ten dollars and forty-five cents with tax," the saleslady said.

Penelope paid for the skates.

She went outside, put them on, and started skating home. She still wished she was old enough to drive a car or rich enough to own a bicycle.

When she got home her mom and dad were in the kitchen.

"I didn't have enough money for a bicycle," she said. "All I could afford were roller skates."

"But roller skates are the best wheels a kid can have," said her dad.

Penelope shoved one of the skates across the floor. "Skating is better than walking, but I'd still rather have a bike."

The next day everyone was going to the ball park to see

Slugger Jones hit his five-hundredth home run. Slugger Jones was

Penelope's favorite ballplayer, and she was going, too.

As she sat on the steps putting on her roller skates, Mr. Smith

came out of his house and got into his car.

"Are you going to the game?" Penelope asked.

"Sure am," answered Mr. Smith.

"I'm skating to the game," said Penelope.

"Be sure you don't get any speeding tickets," he said, and he drove off.

Penelope skated toward the ball park. Her friend Jim rode by on his bicycle.

"Going to the game?" she asked.

"Yep," he said.

"I am too," said Penelope.

"Let's race," said Jim.

Penelope skated as fast as she could, but Jim got ahead of her. Soon she couldn't see him at all.

Penelope skated fast for six blocks and then stopped. Cars were lined up waiting to get into the parking lot.

Penelope skated past Mr. Smith. "I didn't get any speeding tickets," she said.

"Really!" said Mr. Smith.

Near the entrance to the ball park Penelope saw Jim looking

for a place to lock his bike. She skated past him. "Does the winner

get a prize?"

Penelope took off her skates, strapped them together, and waited in line to buy her ticket.

Then she went straight to her favorite seat in the grandstand.

Soon everyone stood up and sang the national anthem. The
umpire yelled, "PLAY BALL!"
Jim walked by looking for a seat.

During the second inning Mr. Smith came in.

Penelope giggled and said, "Roller skates are the best wheels a kid can have."

E   Peterson, Esther
Pet   Allen

        Penelope gets wheels

DATE		
JAN 6 & DEC ... JAN 14 SEP 20		SEP 19 2002
SEP 2 0 1990 MAY 06 92 DEC. 91990		MAY 19 02
OCT 1 3 1990 OCT 1 90 APR. 3 1998		JAN 6 00
FEB 13 MAY 5 MAY 2 0 1998		
MAY		

DATE DUE		
MAR 6 0		
J OCT 822		
4004		